AWESOME DINOSAUR Activities

Mazes, Hidden Pictures, Word Searches, Secret Codes and More!

Diana Zourelias

DOVER PUBLICATIONS
Garden City, New York

Calling all dino-crazed kids! Get to know pterodactyls, T. rexes, triceratops, and many more prehistoric favorites in this fun-filled book. The awesome activities include mazes, hidden pictures, secret codes, spot the differences, word searches, and many other mind-boggling puzzles and brain games. Perfect for after school, weekend, or on-the-go fun! Solutions are included beginning on page 53.

Bibliographical Note
Awesome Dinosaur Activities: Mazes, Hidden Pictures, Word Searches, Secret Codes and More! is a new work, first published by Dover Publications in 2023.

International Standard Book Number
ISBN-13: 978-0-486-85031-3
ISBN-10: 0-486-85031-5

Manufactured in the United States of America
811
www.doverpublications.com

CAN I KEEP HIM?

Can you find the 20 hidden objects in this picture? Cup ◆ Cotton candy
◆ Banana ◆ Lamp ◆ Comb ◆ Pie slice ◆ Sailboat ◆ Crayon ◆ Flag ◆ Moon
◆ Ring ◆ Kite ◆ Wishbone ◆ Stick of gum ◆ Candy cane ◆ Book ◆ Lightning
bolt ◆ Bat ◆ Sock ◆ Star

SPOT THE DIFFERENCE

Find the 7 differences between the top picture and the bottom one.

COLOR BY NUMBER

**COLOR KEY: 1 = Orange 2 = Light Blue 3 = Blue Green 4 = Blue
5 = Yellow Green 6 = Green 7 = Dark Green 8 = Lilac 9 = Brown
No Number = White**

3

IT'S DINOSAUR BEACH DAY!

It's dinosaur beach day! Fill in each blank word bubble
with the word that best describes the action shown.
They all rhyme with the word SHORE!

4

CHOOSE FROM THESE WORDS:
1. FOUR 2. CORE 3. CHORE 4. OAR 5. BOAR 6. DOOR
7. POUR 8. ROAR 9. SNORE 10. STORE

SEARCHOSAURUS

```
N V P M T E X T I N C T Y X C A C
P E S U P L E S M K D A K M C R I
L S Y Z R D B H Z Y N G H B Z M J
A M N K V X R G E F I V C J M O V
T J K L T N O O C R E S T W E R R
E B J Q Y T N S Y E S G X P J Q V
S L P R R H T P T H E R O P O D B
E R B P A N O I S D Z M T A V W T
G I M D N O S K U X D A R F V V W
G F S A N F A E R C L A W S M V M
S R A G O O U S T R I A S S I C U
H I U I S S R F Q J G I Y A R E S
O L R N A S U K Z G I M P T P N E
R L O K U I S M V J L L P C Q Q U
N T P G R L M F Q A O C I U G C M
S X O O U H D I G U A N O D O N D
F J D Z S H L W U W S I H C D K W
```

1. ARMOR	7. PLATES	13. TYRANNOSAURUS
2. EGGS	8. TRIASSIC	14. BRONTOSAURUS
3. MUSEUM	9. CREST	15. CLAWS
4. SPIKES	10. GINKGO	16. IGUANODON
5. EXTINCT	11. FOSSIL	17. SAUROPOD
6. HORNS	12. FRILL	18. THEROPOD

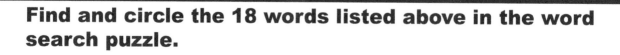

Find and circle the 18 words listed above in the word search puzzle.

1. WHAT DO YOU CALL TWIN DINOSAURS?
2. WHAT'S A SLEEPY DINOSAUR CALLED?
3. WHY DO DINOSAURS EAT RAW MEAT?
4. WHAT HAS 3 HORNS AND 4 WHEELS?
5. WHY WAS THE STEGOSAURUS SUCH A GOOD VOLLEYBALL PLAYER?
6. WHAT DO YOU CALL A DINOSAUR THAT DOESN'T TAKE A BATH?

A. STEGO-SNORE-US
B. BECAUSE HE COULD REALLY SPIKE THE BALL!
C. A TRICERATOPS ON A SKATEBOARD
D. PAIR-ODACTYLS
E. STINK-OSAURUS
F. BECAUSE THEY CAN'T COOK!

1-____ 2-____ 3-____ 4-____ 5-____ 6-____

Can you match the right punch line to each dinosaur joke?
Write the letter of the one you think works best on each line.

LUNCHTIME!

Can you find the 14 hidden objects in this picture? Pencil
◆ Hand ◆ Zipper ◆ Heart ◆ Ring ◆ Bell ◆ Shoe ◆ Mushroom
◆ Cupcake ◆ Licorice twist ◆ Peanut ◆ Wishbone ◆ Crown ◆ Banana

DO THE MATH

Dinosaurs walked on either 2 or 4 feet. Add up the dinosaur feet pictured above to solve each math problem.

WHAT'S DIFFERENT?

The Quetzalcoatlus is the largest known flying creature to have ever lived. It had an incredible 40-foot wingspan and was as tall as a giraffe.

This scene might look like the one on the opposite page, but 10 things have changed. Can you find them?

THE DINO DINER

Draw what the dinosaurs are eating on their blank plates. Hint: Dinosaurs with pointy teeth ate meat. Dinosaurs with rounded teeth ate plants.

DINOSAUR FOOTPRINTS

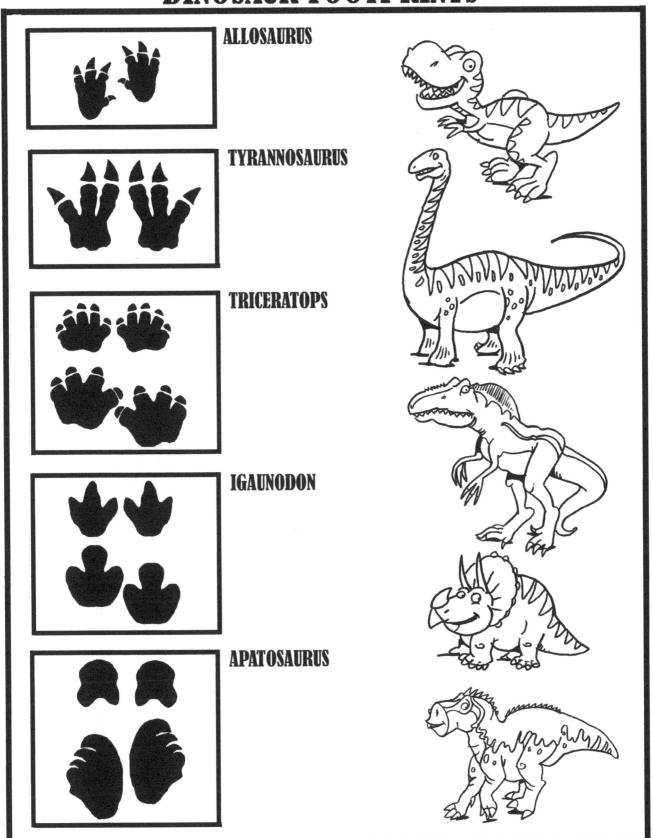

ALLOSAURUS

TYRANNOSAURUS

TRICERATOPS

IGAUNODON

APATOSAURUS

Draw lines that match each dinosaur to its correct footprints.

13

ROUND AND ROUND WE GO

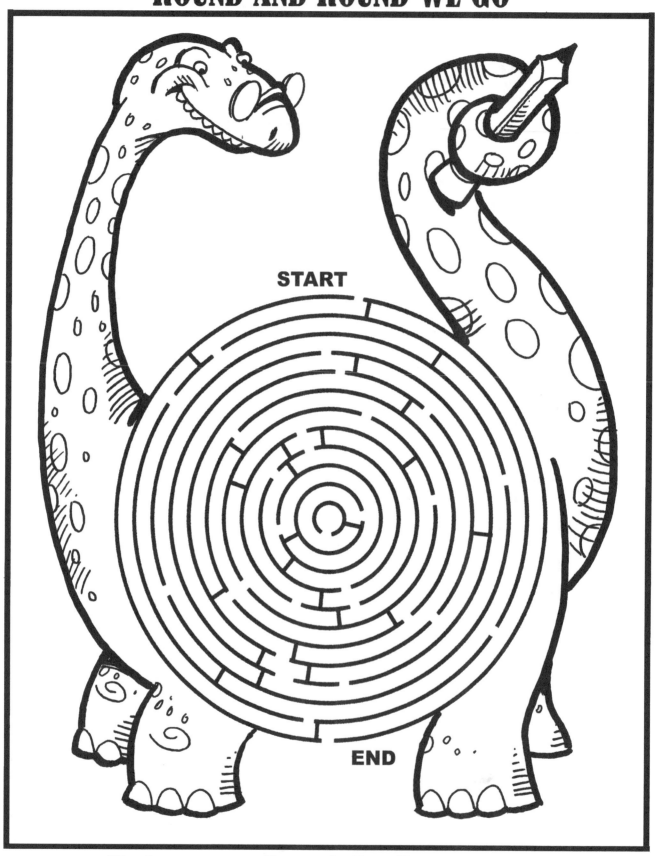

START

END

Find your way through the dinosaur maze.

CRISSCROSS

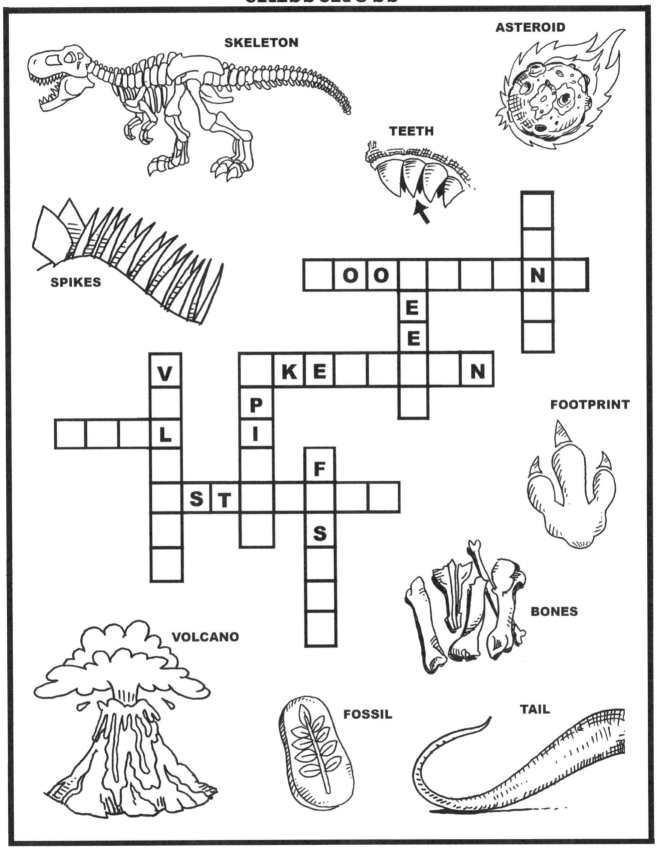

SKELETON

ASTEROID

TEETH

SPIKES

FOOTPRINT

VOLCANO

BONES

FOSSIL

TAIL

Finish writing each word in its correct spot in the puzzle grid.

HOW TO DRAW AN EORAPTOR

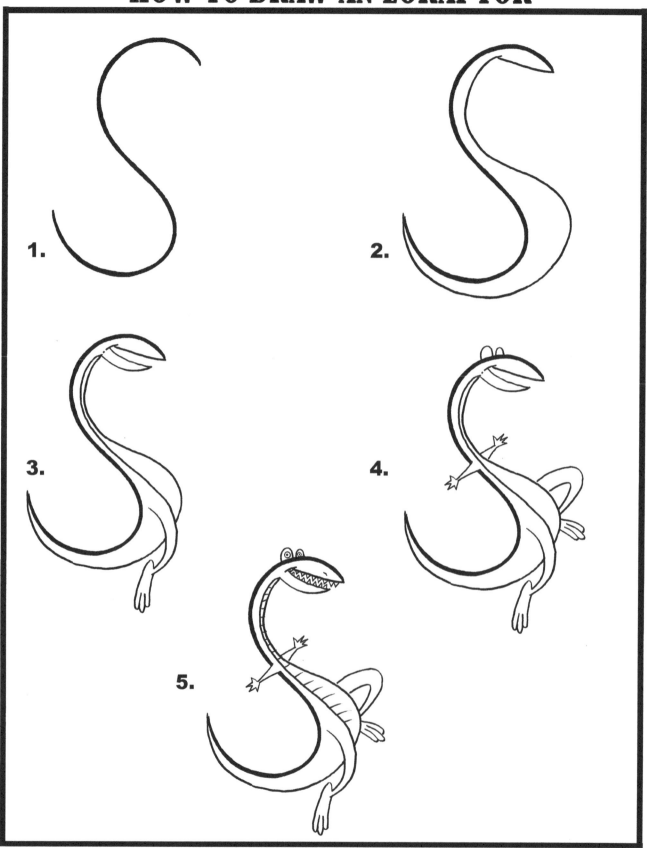

1.

2.

3.

4.

5.

Eoraptors were small carnivorous dinosaurs about the size of a chicken. Follow the 5 steps to draw one on your own. Use the opposite page to practice.

Practice Page

FIND THE BLOOPERS!

DINOSAUR DINOSAUR DINOSAUR DINOSAUR
DINOSAUR DINOSAUR DINOSAUR DINOSAUR
DINOSAUR DINOSAUR DINOSUAR DINOSAUR
DINOSAUR DINOSAUR DINOSAUR DINOSAUR
DINOSAUR DINOSAUR DINOSAUR DINOSAUR
DINOSAUR DINOSAUR DINOSAUR DINOSAUR
DINOSAUR DINOSAUR DINOSAUR DINOSAUR
DINOSAUR DINOSAUR DINOSAUR DINOSAUR
DINOSAUR DINOSAUR DINOSAUR DINOSAUR
DINOSAUR DINOSAUR DINOSAUR DINOSAUR
DINOSAUR DINOSAUR DINOSAUR DINOSAUR
DINOSAUR DINOSAUR DINOSAUR DINOSAUR
DINOSAUR DINOSAUR DINOSAUR DINOSAUR
DINOSAUR DINOSAUR DINOSAUR DINOSAUR
DINOSAUR DIMOSAUR DINOSAUR DINOSAUR
DINOSAUR DINOSAUR DINOSAUR DINOSAUR
DINOSAUR DINOSAUR DINOSAUR DINOSAUR
DINOSAUR DINOSAUR DINOSAUR DINOSAUR
DINOSAUR DINOSAUR DINOSAUR DINOSAUR
DINOSAUR DINOSAUR DINOSAUR DINOSAUR
DINOSAUR DINOSAUR DINOSAUR DINOSAUR
DINOSAUR DINOSAUR DINASUAR DINOSAUR
DINOSAUR DINOSAUR DINOSAUR DINOSAUR
DINOSAUR DINOSAUR DINOSAUR DINOSAUR
DINOSAUR DINOSAUR DINOSAUR DINOSAUR
DINOSAUR DINOSAUR DINOSAUR DINOSAUR
DINOSAUR DINOSAUR DINOSAUR DINOSAUR

Find the 3 misspelled words.

RIDDLE FUN!

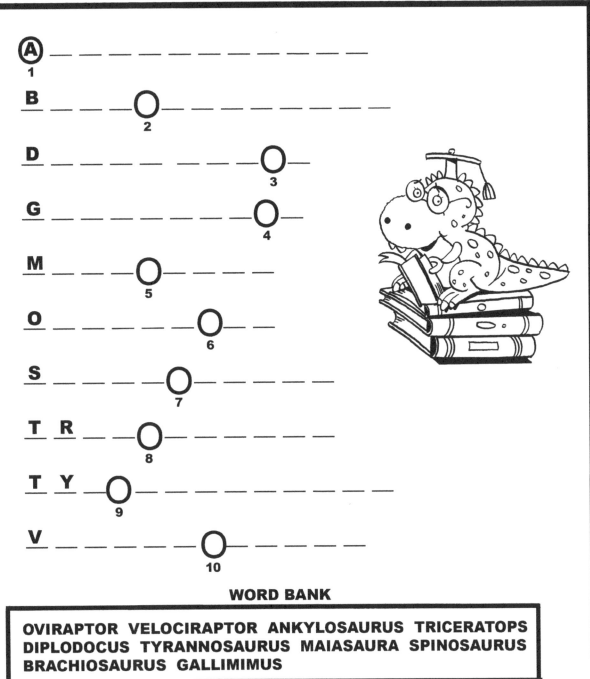

Ⓐ — — — — — — — — — — —
1

B _ — — Ⓞ — — — — — — — —
2

D _ — — — — — Ⓞ — — —
3

G _ — — — — Ⓞ — —
4

M _ — — Ⓞ — — — — —
5

O _ — — — Ⓞ — — — —
6

S _ — — — Ⓞ — — — — —
7

T R — Ⓞ — — — — — — —
8

T Y Ⓞ — — — — — — — —
9

V _ — — — Ⓞ — — — — —
10

WORD BANK

| OVIRAPTOR VELOCIRAPTOR ANKYLOSAURUS TRICERATOPS |
| DIPLODOCUS TYRANNOSAURUS MAIASAURA SPINOSAURUS |
| BRACHIOSAURUS GALLIMIMUS |

What do you call a dinosaur with a huge vocabulary?

— — — — — — — — — — —
1   6   2   8   5   9   3   10   4   7

Finish writing the words from the word bank in alphabetical order on the lines. Then write each circled letter on its matching numbered line to spell out the answer to the riddle.

DINOSAUR

2-LETTER WORDS

_____

_____

_____

_____

_____

_____

_____

_____

3-LETTER WORDS

_____

_____

_____

_____

_____

_____

_____

_____

4-LETTER WORDS

_____   _____

_____   _____

_____   _____

_____   _____

How many 2-, 3-, and 4-letter words can you make from the word DINOSAUR?

FIND IT! COLOR IT!

The pterodactyls are having a fish fry! An ANKYLOSAURUS is hidden in the picture. Can you find it?

ME AND MY SHADOW

A. GALLIMIMUS

B. ALLOSAURUS

C. STEGOSAURUS

D. PARASAUROLOPHUS

E. APATOSAURUS

F. PACHYCEPHALOSAURUS

Match each dinosaur on this page with its shadow on the opposite page. Write the correct letter on the blanks provided.

YOU'RE THE ARTIST!

**Draw a funny (or scary) dinosaur in the open space.
Then color the picture.**

SEARCHOSAURUS

```
H V D S N C A R N I V O R E Y
H L E I M I S U P E N D S O Y
N P U L P A N W H L B I K B B
P U R S O L M F U V O N E R J
J T K E T C O M Z I N O L F T
J G E D H E I D O C E S E O R
U L E R F I G R O T S A T O I
R T G O O O S O A C H U O T C
A R X L L D S T S P U R N P E
S E U F Z O A S O A T S C R R
S X V J N W G C I R U O W I A
I U B Q Z D C I T L I R R N T
C D L J U C D S S Y Z C U T O
X H V O L C A N O T L E T S P
Q A V G H E R B I V O R E N S
```

1. FOSSIL
2. DINOSAUR
3. FOOTPRINT
4. VOLCANO
5. GEOLOGIST
6. T. REX
7. PTERODACTYL
8. HERBIVORE
9. DIPLODOCUS
10. TRICERATOPS
11. STEGOSAURUS
12. VELOCIRAPTOR
13. BONES
14. MAMMOTH
15. JURASSIC
16. SKELETON
17. CARNIVORE
18. PREHISTORIC

Find and circle the 18 words listed above in the word search puzzle.

WHAT'S DIFFERENT?

This dinosaur loves to paint pictures of his favorite things!

This scene might look like the one on the opposite page, but 10 things have changed. Can you find them?

CODE CRUSHER

_ _ _ _ _ _ Ⓞ _ _ _ _ _   _ _ _ Ⓞ _
W Y X U O I   Z E J J V O   D B O O C

_ _ Ⓞ _ _ _ _ _   Ⓞ _ _ _ _ _
M Y X S P O B C   M I M K N C

_ _ _ _ _ _ _ Ⓞ Ⓞ _   _ _ _ _ Ⓞ
R Y B C O D K S V C   P O B X C

CODE

A=Q B=R C=S D=T E=U F=V G=W
H=X I=Y J=Z K=A L=B M=C N=D
O=E P=F Q=G R=H S=I T=J U=K
V=L W=M X=N Y=O Z=P

The diplodocus was a herbivore that ate hundreds of pounds of greens each day! His teeth were the shape of . . .

_ _ _ _ _ _ _ .

What kinds of plants did herbivores eat? Use the code to find out. Then write the circled letters, in order, on the blank lines to finish the sentence.

LAUGH-O-SAURUS

1. WHAT DO YOU GET WHEN A DINOSAUR CRASHES ITS CAR?
2. WHAT'S THE NAME OF THE FASTEST DINOSAUR?
3. HOW DO YOU KNOW IF A DINOSAUR IS IN YOUR REFRIGERATOR?
4. WHAT GAME DOES A BRONTOSAURUS LIKE TO PLAY WITH HUMANS?
5. WHICH DINOSAUR CAN JUMP HIGHER THAN A HOUSE?
6. WHEN CAN 3 LARGE DINOSAURS HIDE UNDER A LITTLE UMBRELLA AND NOT GET WET?

A. WHEN IT'S NOT RAINING!
B. PRONTO-SAURUS
C. SQUASH
D. THE DOOR WON'T SHUT!
E. A TYRANNOSAURUS WRECK
F. ANY DINOSAUR—A HOUSE CAN'T JUMP!

1- ____ 2- ____ 3- ____ 4- ____ 5- ____ 6- ____

Can you match the right punch line to each dinosaur joke? Write the letter of the one you think works best on each line.

PLESIOSAUR WATER MAZE

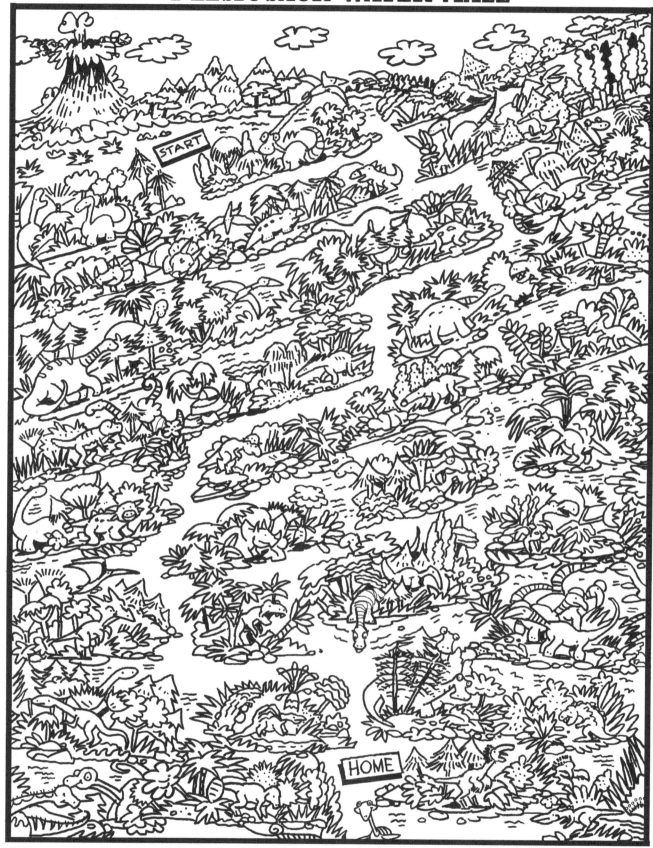

The plesiosaur was a swimming dinosaur. Help this one travel through the maze to get home.

FIND MY TWIN

The baby dinosaur circled at the top is looking for his identical twin. Find and circle his match.

FIND IT! COLOR IT!

The little dinosaurs are having fun! There is a **TRICERATOPS** hidden in the picture. Can you find it?

SALAD FOR LUNCH

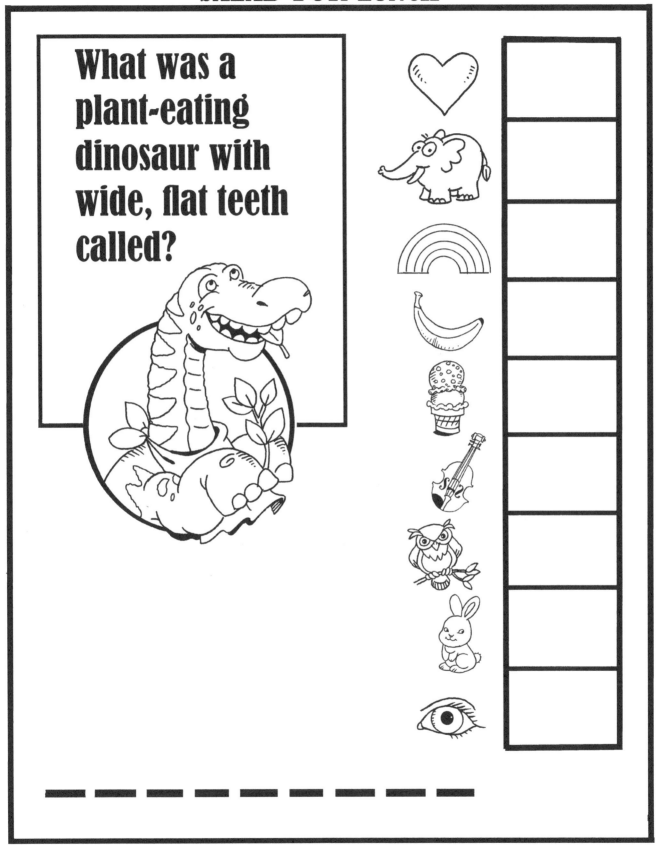

What was a plant-eating dinosaur with wide, flat teeth called?

Write the first letter of each picture clue in the corresponding box. Then write those letters, in order, on the blank lines to find the answer.

YOU'RE THE ARTIST

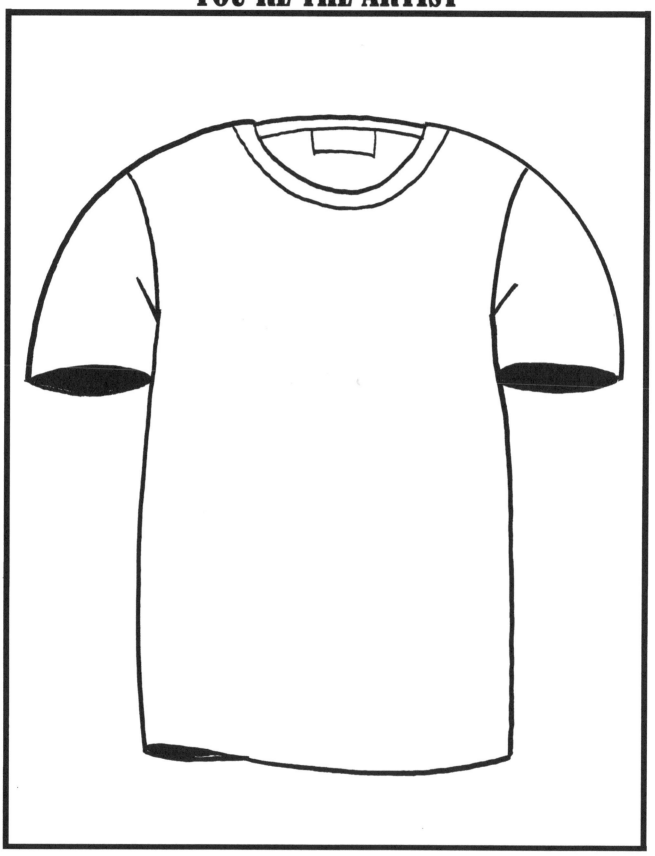

Create a dinosaur design for a T-shirt you would wear!

TWO OF A KIND

_____and_____

_____and_____

_____and_____

_____and_____

_____and_____

_____and_____

Can you find the 6 pairs of identical twin dinosaurs?
Write the letters of the twins on the blank lines.

FIND THE MAMASAURUS

A.

B.

C.

D.

A baby dinosaur is about to come out of its shell! Follow the different wiggly lines to find the mamasaurus.

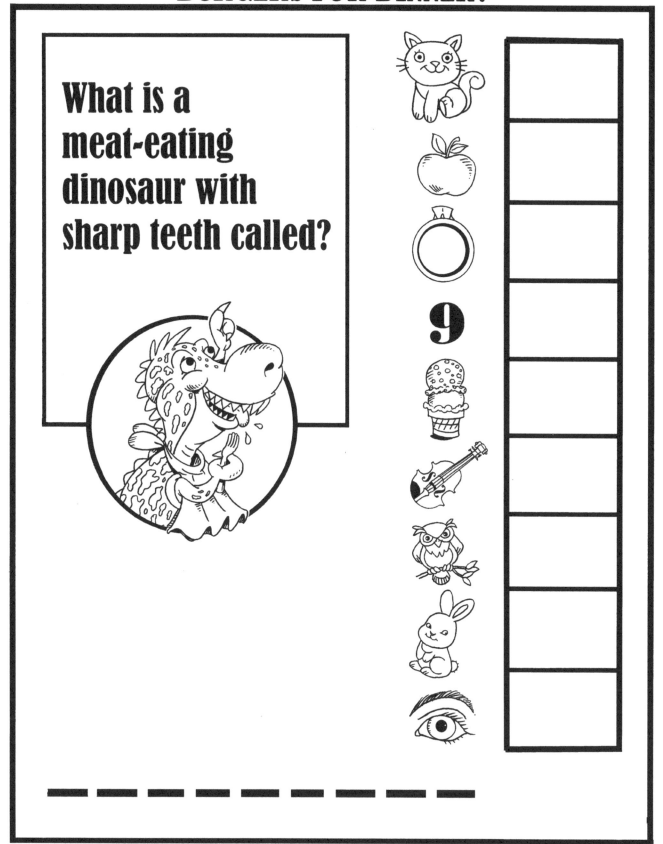

What is a meat-eating dinosaur with sharp teeth called?

_ _ _ _ _ _ _ _ _

Write the first letter of each picture clue in the corresponding box. Then write those letters, in order, on the blank lines to find the answer.

D IS FOR DINOSAUR

Find and color the 10 capital *D*'s hidden in this picture.

SPOT THE DIFFERENCE

Find the 7 differences between the top picture and the bottom one.

FIND THE BLOOPERS!

FOSSILS FOSSILS FOSSILS FOSSILS FOSSILS FOSSILS
FOSSILS FOSSILS FOSSILS FOSSILS FOSSILS FOSSILS
FOSSILS FOSSILS FOSSILS FOSSILS FOSSILS FOSSILS
FOSSILS FOSSILS FOSSILS FOSSILS FOSSILS FOSSILS
FOSSILS FOSSILS FOSSILS FOSSILS FOSSILS FOSSILS
FOSSILS FOSSILS FOSSILS FOSSILS FOSSILS FOSSILS
FOSSILS FOSSILS FOSSILS FOSSILS FOSSILS FOSSILS
FOSSILS FOSSILS FOSSILS FOSSILS FOSSILS FOSSILS
FOSSILS FOSSILS FOSSILS FOSSILS FOSSILS FOSSILS
FOSSILS FOSSILS FOSSILS FOSSILS FOSSILS FOSSILS
FOSSILS FOSSILS FOSSILS FOSSILS FOSSILS FOSSILS
FOSSILS FOSSILS FOSSILS FOSSILS EOSSILS FOSSILS
FOSSILS FOSSILS FOSSILS FOSSILS FOSSILS FOSSILS
FOSSILS FOSSILS FOSSILS FOSSILS FOSSILS FOSSILS
FOSSILS FOSSILS FOSSILS FOSSILS FOSSILS FOSSILS
FOSSILS FOSSILS FOSSILS FOSSILS FOSSILS FOSSILS
FOSSILS FOSSILS FOSSILS FOSSILS FOSSILS FOSSILS
FOSSILS FOSSILS FOSSILS FOSSILS FOSSILS FOSSILS
FOSSILS FOZZILS FOSSILS FOSSILS FOSSILS FOSSILS
FOSSILS FOSSILS FOSSILS FOSSILS FOSSILS FOSSILS
FOSSILS FOSSILS FOSSILS FOSSILS FOSSILS FOSSILS
FOSSILS FOSSILS FOSSILS FOSSILS FOSSILS FOSSILS
FOSSILS FOSSILS FOSSILS FOSSILS FOSSILS FOSSILS
FOSSILS FOSSILS FOSSILS FOSSILS FOSSILS FOSSILS
FOSSILS FOSSILS FOSSILS FOSSILS FUSSILS FOSSILS
FOSSILS FOSSILS FOSSILS FOSSILS FOSSILS FOSSILS
FOSSILS FOSSILS FOSSILS FOSSILS FOSSILS FOSSILS
FOSSILS FOSSILS FOSSILS FOSSILS FOSSILS FOSSILS
FOSSILS FOSSILS FOSSILS FOSSILS FOSSILS FOSSILS
FOSSILS FOSSILS FOSSILS FOSSILS FOSSILS FOSSILS

Find the 3 misspelled words.

DOTTY DINOSAUR

Connect the dots from 1 to 100 to draw the funny dinosaur.

WHAT'S IN A NAME?

The word DINOSAUR comes from the Greek words *deinos* and *sauros*. What do they mean?

Cross out the first letter and every other letter after that.

J T M E F R H
R N I T B Z L
C E U L D I Q
Z Y A N R F D

Write the remaining letters below, in the order that they appear, to spell the answer.

- - - - - - - -
- - - - - -

FIND THE IMPOSTOR

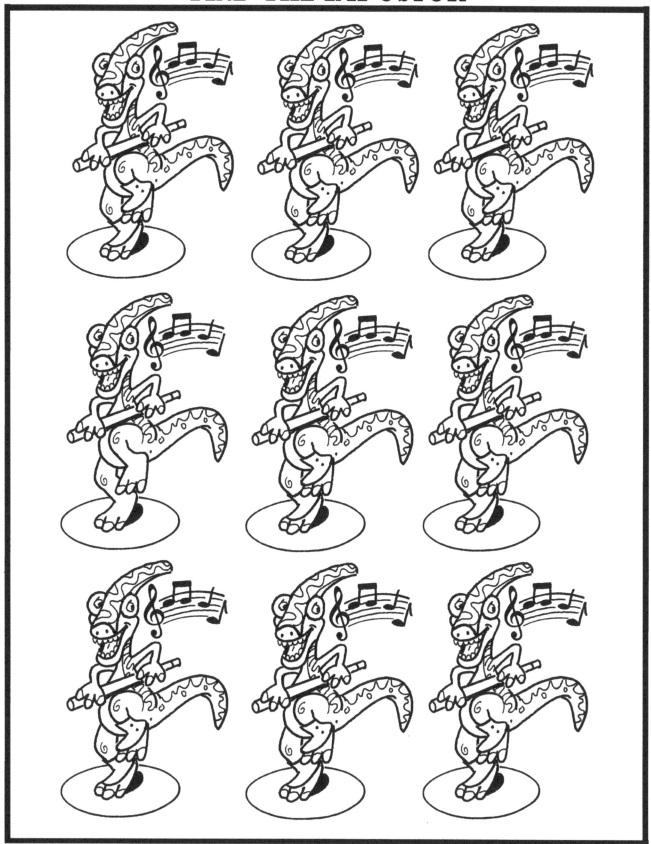

There are 9 dancing dinosaurs in this picture. Can you find the one dinosaur that is different?

TYRANNOSAURUS

2-LETTER WORDS

_____

_____

_____

_____

_____

_____

_____

_____

3-LETTER WORDS

_____

_____

_____

_____

_____

_____

_____

_____

4-LETTER WORDS

_____   _____

_____   _____

_____   _____

_____   _____

How many 2-, 3-, and 4-letter words can you make from the word TYRANNOSAURUS?

CREATE YOUR OWN DINOSAUR NAMES!

1. Write your first or last name on the line below.

_____

2. Write your name again + something about you (special talent, interest, favorite subject, color, food, etc.).

_____

3. Write your name + the first thing you added + one of the following:

   RAPTOR if you eat **ONLY** meat
   OSAURUS if you eat **BOTH** veggies and meat
   OCUS if you eat **ONLY** veggies

   for example: Marymathosaurus or Johnsoccerocus

   your turn: _____

Use the lines below to create special dinosaur names for your family and friends—and even your pets!

_____

_____

_____

_____

DRAW A TRICERATOPS FACE

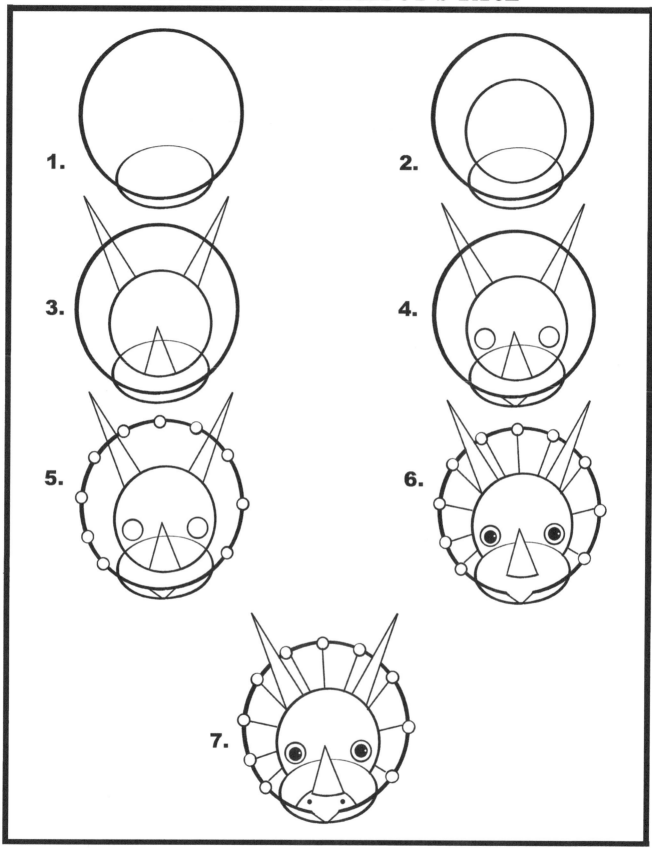

Follow the 7 steps to draw a triceratops face using circles, ovals, and triangles. Use the opposite page to practice.

Practice Page

HOW MANY FEET?

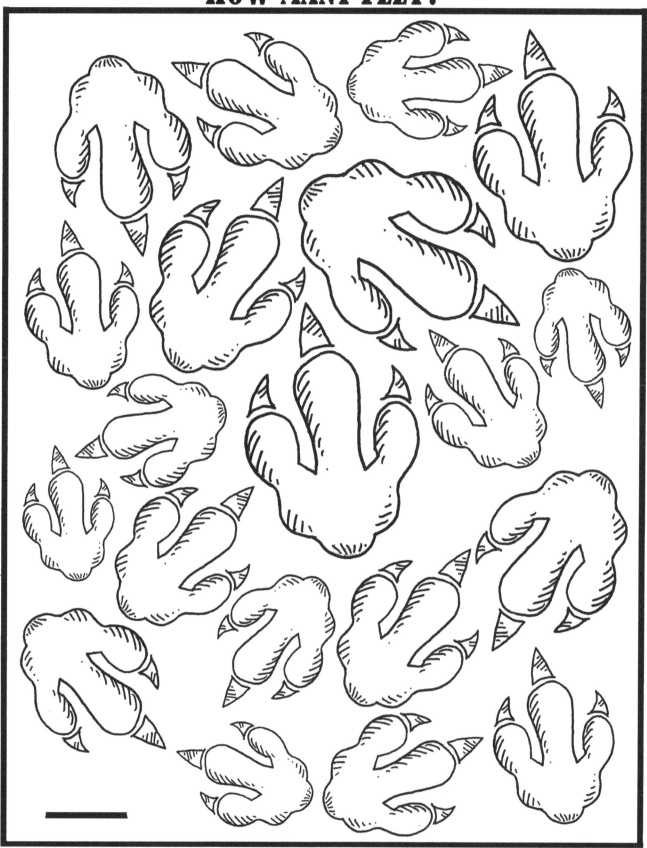

A 3-toed dinosaur is called a theropod. Count the theropod footprints, and write the answer in the blank.

FIND THE TWINS!

Find and circle one set of identical twin dinos.

IT'S AMAZEING!

START

END

See how quickly you can find your way through this dinosaur maze.

SWIM CLASS

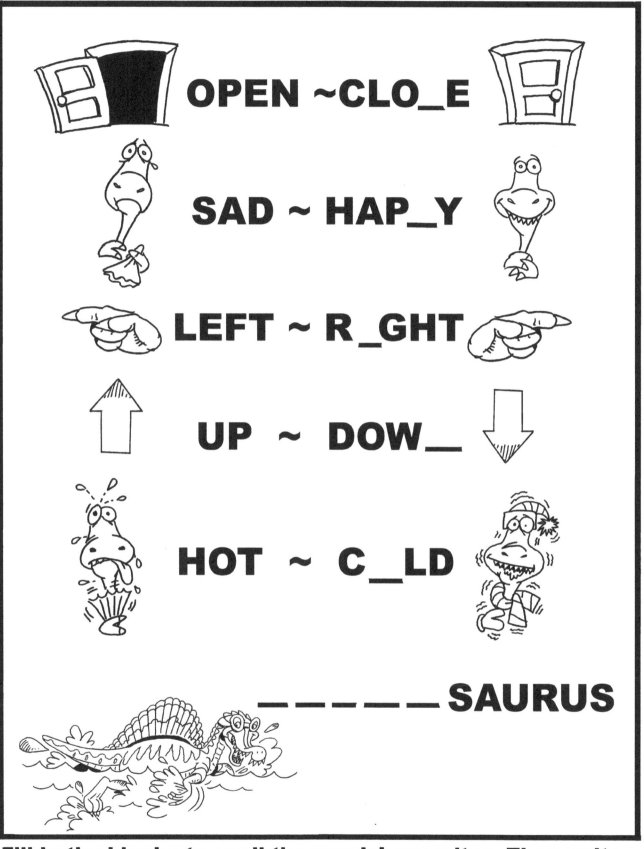

OPEN ~CLO_E

SAD ~ HAP_Y

LEFT ~ R_GHT

UP ~ DOW__

HOT ~ C__LD

__ __ __ __ __ __ SAURUS

Fill in the blanks to spell the words' opposites. Then write the letters you added, from top to bottom, on the blanks below to find the name of a swimming dinosaur.

IT'S A T. REX BIRTHDAY PARTY!

Find and circle these 12 things that start with the letter *T*: TRUMPET, TABLE, TOMATO, TREE, TENNIS SHOES, TEACUP, TOOTHBRUSH, TURTLE, TEDDY BEAR, TIRE, TENT, and TULIP.

SOLUTIONS

CAN I KEEP HIM?

Page 1

SPOT THE DIFFERENCE

Page 2

IT'S DINOSAUR BEACH DAY!

Page 4

SEARCHOSAURUS

```
N V P M T E X T I N C T Y X C A C
P E S U P L E S M K D A K M C R I
L S Y Z R D B H Z Y N G H B Z M J
A M N K V X N G E F I V C J M O V
T J K L T R O C R E S T W E R R J
E B J Q R Y N S Y E S G X P J O B
S L P R A T O P T H E R O P O D V
E R B P M N O S I S D Z M T A V W T
G I M D N A S K U X D A R F V V W
G F S A N F U E R C L A W S M V M
S F R A G I N O U S T R I A S S I C U
H R I L S U R F Q J G I Y A R E S
O L A U R U K Z G I M P T P N E
R L O K G U S M V J L L P C Q Q M
N T X O Z H L M F Q A O C I U G C M
S F J D Z S H L W U W S I H C D K W
```

1. ARMOR	7. PLATES	13. TYRANNOSAURUS
2. EGGS	8. TRIASSIC	14. BRONTOSAURUS
3. MUSEUM	9. CREST	15. CLAWS
4. SPIKES	10. GINKGO	16. IGUANODON
5. EXTINCT	11. FOSSIL	17. SAUROPOD
6. HORNS	12. FRILL	18. THEROPOD

Page 6

LAUGHOSAURUS

1. WHAT DO YOU CALL TWIN DINOSAURS?
2. WHAT'S A SLEEPY DINOSAUR CALLED?
3. WHY DO DINOSAURS EAT RAW MEAT?
4. WHAT HAS 3 HORNS AND 4 WHEELS?
5. WHY WAS THE STEGOSAURUS SUCH A GOOD VOLLEYBALL PLAYER?
6. WHAT DO YOU CALL A DINOSAUR THAT DOESN'T TAKE A BATH?

A. STEGO-SNORE-US
B. BECAUSE HE COULD REALLY SPIKE THE BALL!
C. A TRICERATOPS ON A SKATEBOARD
D. PAIR-ODACTYLS
E. STINK-OSAURUS
F. BECAUSE THEY CAN'T COOK!

__1-D__   __2-A__   __3-F__   __4-C__   __5-B__   __6-E__

Page 7

LUNCHTIME!

Page 8

DO THE MATH

= __12__ FEET

= __14__ FEET

= __8__ FEET

= __14__ FEET

= __16__ FEET

Page 9

WHAT'S DIFFERENT?

Page 10

DINOSAUR FOOTPRINTS

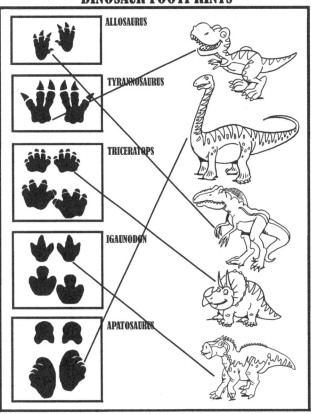

ALLOSAURUS

TYRANNOSAURUS

TRICERATOPS

IGAUNODON

APATOSAURUS

Page 13

ROUND AND ROUND WE GO

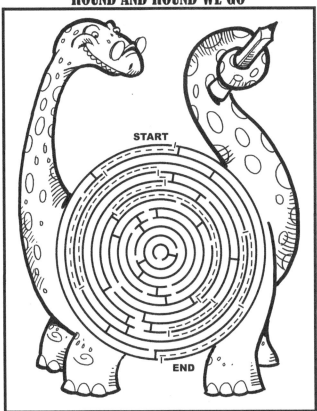

START

END

Page 14

CRISSCROSS

SKELETON

ASTEROID

TEETH

SPIKES

FOOTPRINT

BONES

VOLCANO

FOSSIL

TAIL

Page 15

FIND THE BLOOPERS!

Page 18

DINOSAUR DINOSAUR DINOSAUR DINOSAUR
DINOSAUR DINOSAUR DINOSAUR DINOSAUR
DINOSAUR DINOSAUR DINOSUAR DINOSAUR
DINOSAUR DINOSAUR DINOSAUR DINOSAUR
DINOSAUR DINOSAUR DINOSAUR DINOSAUR
DINOSAUR DINOSAUR DINOSAUR DINOSAUR
DINOSAUR DINOSAUR DINOSAUR DINOSAUR
DINOSAUR DINOSAUR DINOSAUR DINOSAUR
DINOSAUR DINOSAUR DINOSAUR DINOSAUR
DINOSAUR DINOSAUR DINOSAUR DINOSAUR
DINOSAUR DINOSAUR DINOSAUR DINOSAUR
DINOSAUR DINOSAUR DINOSAUR DINOSAUR
DINOSAUR DINOSAUR DINOSAUR DINOSAUR
DINOSAUR DINOSAUR DINOSAUR DINOSAUR
DINOSAUR DIMOSAUR DINOSAUR DINOSAUR
DINOSAUR DINOSAUR DINOSAUR DINOSAUR
DINOSAUR DINOSAUR DINOSAUR DINOSAUR
DINOSAUR DINOSAUR DINOSAUR DINOSAUR
DINOSAUR DINOSAUR DINOSAUR DINOSAUR
DINOSAUR DINOSAUR DINOSAUR DINOSAUR
DINOSAUR DINOSAUR DINASUAR DINOSAUR
DINOSAUR DINOSAUR DINOSAUR DINOSAUR
DINOSAUR DINOSAUR DINOSAUR DINOSAUR
DINOSAUR DINOSAUR DINOSAUR DINOSAUR
DINOSAUR DINOSAUR DINOSAUR DINOSAUR

RIDDLE FUN!

Page 19

A N K Y L O S A U R U S
1

B R A C H I O S A U R U S
2

D I P L O D O C U S
3

G A L L I M I M U S
4

M A I A S A U R A
5

O V I R A P T O R
6

S P I N O S A U R U S
7

T R I C E R A T O P S
8

T Y R A N N O S A U R U S
9

V E L O C I R A P T O R
10

WORD BANK

OVIRAPTOR VELOCIRAPTOR ANKYLOSAURUS TRICERATOPS
DIPLODOCUS TYRANNOSAURUS MAIASAURA SPINOSAURUS
BRACHIOSAURUS GALLIMIMUS

What do you call a dinosaur with a huge vocabulary?

A   T H E S A U R U S
1   6 2 8 5 9 3 10 4 7

DINOSAUR

Page 20

2-LETTER WORDS	3-LETTER WORDS
AD	AIR
AN	AND
AS	NOD
DO	OUR
IN	RAN
IS	ROD
ON	SAD
NO	SIR
SO	SON
US	SUN

4-LETTER WORDS

IRON	SAID
RAIN	SAND
ROAD	SOAR
RUNS	SODA

FIND IT! COLOR IT!

Page 21

FISH FRY

ME AND MY SHADOW

Page 22

SEARCHOSAURUS

1. FOSSIL
2. DINOSAUR
3. FOOTPRINT
4. VOLCANO
5. GEOLOGIST
6. T. REX
7. PTERODACTYL
8. HERBIVORE
9. DIPLODOCUS
10. TRICERATOPS
11. STEGOSAURUS
12. VELOCIRAPTOR
13. BONES
14. MAMMOTH
15. JURASSIC
16. SKELETON
17. CARNIVORE
18. PREHISTORIC

Page 25

WHAT'S DIFFERENT?

Page 26

CODE CRUSHER

<u>M</u><u>O</u><u>N</u><u>K</u><u>E</u><u>Y</u> (P)<u>U</u><u>Z</u><u>Z</u><u>L</u><u>E</u> T<u>R</u><u>E</u>(E)<u>S</u>

<u>C</u><u>O</u>(N)<u>I</u><u>F</u><u>E</u><u>R</u><u>S</u> (C)<u>Y</u><u>C</u><u>A</u><u>D</u><u>S</u>

<u>H</u><u>O</u><u>R</u><u>S</u><u>E</u><u>T</u><u>A</u>(I)<u>L</u><u>S</u> <u>F</u><u>E</u><u>R</u><u>N</u>(S)

CODE

A=Q B=R C=S D=T E=U F=V G=W
H=X I=Y J=Z K=A L=B M=C N=D
O=E P=F Q=G R=H S=I T=J U=K
V=L W=M X=N Y=O Z=P

The diplodocus was a herbivore that ate hundreds of pounds of greens each day! His teeth were the shape of . . .

<u>P</u> <u>E</u> <u>N</u> <u>C</u> <u>I</u> <u>L</u> <u>S</u> .

Page 28

LAUGH-O-SAURUS

1. WHAT DO YOU GET WHEN A DINOSAUR CRASHES ITS CAR?
2. WHAT'S THE NAME OF THE FASTEST DINOSAUR?
3. HOW DO YOU KNOW IF A DINOSAUR IS IN YOUR REFRIGERATOR?
4. WHAT GAME DOES A BRONTOSAURUS LIKE TO PLAY WITH HUMANS?
5. WHICH DINOSAUR CAN JUMP HIGHER THAN A HOUSE?
6. WHEN CAN 3 LARGE DINOSAURS HIDE UNDER A LITTLE UMBRELLA AND NOT GET WET?

A. WHEN IT'S NOT RAINING!
B. PRONTO-SAURUS
C. SQUASH
D. THE DOOR WON'T SHUT!
E. A TYRANNOSAURUS WRECK
F. ANY DINOSAUR—A HOUSE CAN'T JUMP!

1-E   2-B   3-D   4-C   5-F   6-A

Page 29

PLESIOSAUR WATER MAZE

Page 30

FIND MY TWIN

Page 31

FIND IT! COLOR IT!

Page 32

SALAD FOR LUNCH

What was a plant-eating dinosaur with wide, flat teeth called?

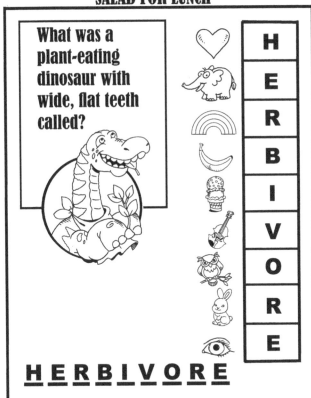

H E R B I V O R E

TWO OF A KIND

A ___ and ___ K
C ___ and ___ L
E ___ and ___ G

B ___ and ___ H
D ___ and ___ I
F ___ and ___ J

FIND THE MAMASAURUS

BURGERS FOR DINNER?

What is a meat-eating dinosaur with sharp teeth called?

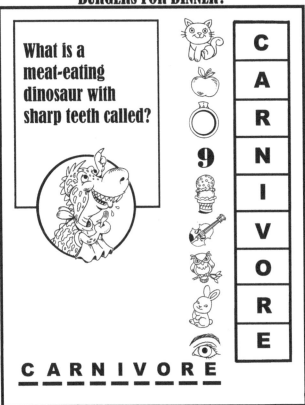

C A R N I V O R E

D IS FOR DINOSAUR

Page 38

SPOT THE DIFFERENCE

Page 39

FIND THE BLOOPERS!

FOSSILS FOSSILS FOSSILS FOSSILS FOSSILS FOSSILS
FOSSILS FOSSILS FOSSILS FOSSILS FOSSILS FOSSILS
FOSSILS FOSSILS FOSSILS FOSSILS FOSSILS FOSSILS
FOSSILS FOSSILS FOSSILS FOSSILS FOSSILS FOSSILS
FOSSILS FOSSILS FOSSILS FOSSILS FOSSILS FOSSILS
FOSSILS FOSSILS FOSSILS FOSSILS FOSSILS FOSSILS
FOSSILS FOSSILS FOSSILS FOSSILS FOSSILS FOSSILS
FOSSILS FOSSILS FOSSILS FOSSILS FOSSILS FOSSILS
FOSSILS FOSSILS FOSSILS FOSSILS FOSSILS FOSSILS
FOSSILS FOSSILS FOSSILS FOSSILS FOSSILS FOSSILS
FOSSILS FOSSILS FOSSILS FOSSILS FOSSILS FOSSILS
FOSSILS FOSSILS FOSSILS FOSSILS EOSSILS FOSSILS
FOSSILS FOSSILS FOSSILS FOSSILS FOSSILS FOSSILS
FOSSILS FOSSILS FOSSILS FOSSILS FOSSILS FOSSILS
FOSSILS FOSSILS FOSSILS FOSSILS FOSSILS FOSSILS
FOSSILS FOSSILS FOSSILS FOSSILS FOSSILS FOSSILS
FOSSILS FOSSILS FOSSILS FOSSILS FOSSILS FOSSILS
FOSSILS FOSSILS FOSSILS FOSSILS FOSSILS FOSSILS
FOSSILS FOZZILS FOSSILS FOSSILS FOSSILS FOSSILS
FOSSILS FOSSILS FOSSILS FOSSILS FOSSILS FOSSILS
FOSSILS FOSSILS FOSSILS FOSSILS FOSSILS FOSSILS
FOSSILS FOSSILS FOSSILS FOSSILS FOSSILS FOSSILS
FOSSILS FOSSILS FOSSILS FOSSILS FOSSILS FOSSILS
FOSSILS FOSSILS FOSSILS FOSSILS FUSSILS FOSSILS
FOSSILS FOSSILS FOSSILS FOSSILS FOSSILS FOSSILS
FOSSILS FOSSILS FOSSILS FOSSILS FOSSILS FOSSILS
FOSSILS FOSSILS FOSSILS FOSSILS FOSSILS FOSSILS
FOSSILS FOSSILS FOSSILS FOSSILS FOSSILS FOSSILS

Page 40

DOTTY DINOSAUR

Page 41

WHAT'S IN A NAME?

The word DINOSAUR comes from the Greek words *deinos* and *sauros*. What do they mean?

Cross out the first letter and every other letter after that.

J T M E F R H
R N I T B Z L
G E U L D I Q
Z X A N R F D

Write the remaining letters below, in the order that they appear, to spell the answer.

T E R R I B L E
L I Z A R D

Page 42

FIND THE IMPOSTOR

Page 43

TYRANNOSAURUS

2-LETTER WORDS	3-LETTER WORDS
AN	ANY
AS	NOT
AT	NUT
NO	OUT
ON	RAN
OR	RAT
SO	SUN
TO	TOY
US	TRY

4-LETTER WORDS

AUNT	STAR
AUTO	STUN
NUTS	TRAY
ROAR	TUNA

Page 44

HOW MANY FEET?

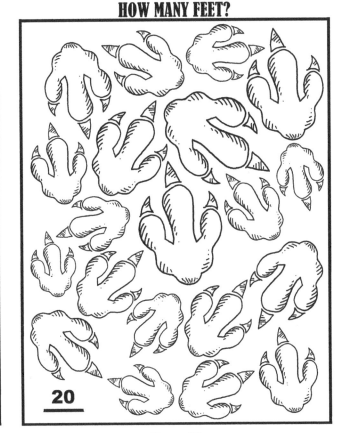

20

Page 48

FIND THE TWINS!

Page 49

IT'S AMAZEING!

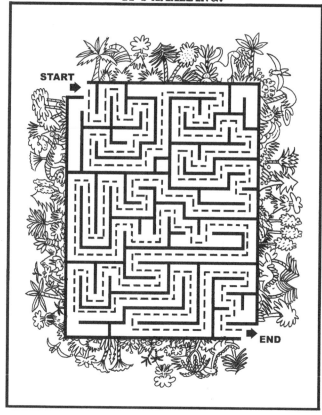

START

END

Page 50

SWIM CLASS

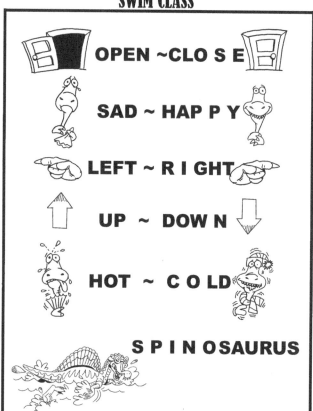

OPEN ~CLO S E

SAD ~ HAP P Y

LEFT ~ R I GHT

UP ~ DOW N

HOT ~ C O LD

S P I N OSAURUS

Page 51

IT'S A T. REX BIRTHDAY PARTY!

ICE CREAM

CORN

MEAT

GIFTS

CLAP

Page 52